Abuelito

Eats With His Fingers

To Rick, with all my love.—J. L.

To my loving wife Sondra, the person who motivates me.
To my Mom and Dad, Avis and O.B., whom I love and respect.
And special thanks to Ashley Massey.
In memory of Herman Hudson, a patient and giving man — a second father to me. —Layne Johnson

FIRST EDITION

Copyright 1999
By Janice Levy

Published in the United States of America
By Eakin Press
A Division of Sunbelt Media, Inc.
P.O. Drawer 90159
Austin, TX 78709

3 4 5 6 7 8 9

ISBN 1-57168-177-9

Printed in Hong Kong

Abuelito
Eats With His Fingers

Janice Levy

Illustrated by Layne Johnson

EAKIN PRESS ★ AUSTIN, TEXAS

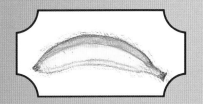

I don't like to visit Abuelito. My grandfather ruins my whole day.

I don't like to look at him. Water leaks out of his eyes. He cuts himself shaving and sticks little pieces of tissue all over his face.

His cheekbones are so high you can rest a coin on them. His nose is too big and his eyes are too small. Nothing on his face fits.

He smells like green library soap or sometimes like fried bananas. Abuelito eats with his fingers.

I don't like Abuelito's house.
Nobody my age plays in the street.
    The furniture in the living room is
covered with plastic. The sofa sticks
to my legs.

    Abuelito lights candles and keeps little statues
in every room. At night, the whole place looks
    spooky. I can't wait to go home.

My friend, Hope, has a grandfather who's famous. He has a swimming pool in his living room. He owns a red Corvette.

Abuelito doesn't know how to drive. That's why we bring him meat from the butcher, in paper bags that leak through the bottom.

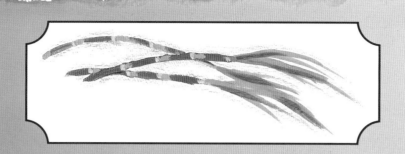

My mother and Abuelito speak in Spanish. My mother translates Abuelito's questions. "Are you studying? Are you obeying your mother?" My mother kicks my foot under the table and I nod my head yes.

"Stay with Abuelito, Tina," my mother says. "I'll be back soon."

"Do I have to?" I ask. "You've never left me with him before."

Abuelito tilts his head like my dog does when I push him off my pillow.

Abuelito touches my face and smiles. His knuckles are bumpy. Hope's grandfather wears a ruby ring. He's never cut sugar cane.

I turn away and walk into Abuelito's bedroom. The walls are covered with black and white photographs. Abuelito looks much younger in his straw hat, holding a fishing pole.

In all the pictures, a woman with long, dark hair stands at his side. My *abuelita*, Cristina, died before I was born. I am named after her.

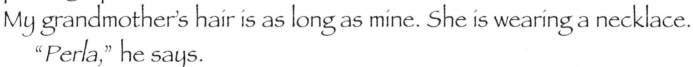

Abuelito points to one of the photographs on his wall.

My grandmother's hair is as long as mine. She is wearing a necklace.

"*Perla*," he says.

Abuelito takes a pearl necklace from a velvet jewelry box. I feel his rough fingers around my neck.

Abuelito shows me a pad
of drawings in colored chalk.
He flips the pages quickly,
so they look like a movie.
I see palm trees and sunsets
the color of fruits. I wonder
what his eyes see now.

Abuelito draws a big heart and a woman with
flowers in her long, dark hair. On the next page
Abuelito draws a church. The woman's dress looks
like snowflakes.

Abuelito smiles and gives me the crayons. I draw
a baby in a crib, then a little girl, then a woman who
looks like my mother. Abuelito puts each page on
the floor in order.

Abuelito draws the dark-haired lady in a fishing boat called *La Cristina,* under a sky of black clouds. He jabs the paper, and raindrops begin to fall like spears. Abuelito scribbles with blue until the whole page looks soaking wet. He rips the paper from the pad and crumples it up. He covers his eyes with his hands.

"What happened to Abuelita Cristina?" I ask. Abuelito doesn't answer.

I draw my face with a smile that looks like a pearl necklace. I write "LOVE" in big letters at the top. Abuelito touches my cheek. He looks at me until I have to turn away.

Abuelito takes my drawing and leans it against one of the statues on a table.

"*Los santos,*" he says and introduces each saint with a little bow. Abuelito lights a candle. He closes his eyes and moves his lips. Abuelito puts an arm around my shoulder. I whisper a prayer for my mother, Abuelito, my friend Hope, and then mostly for me.

When I open my eyes, the statues are in different places. Abuelito winks.

My stomach makes a grumbling noise. Abuelito licks his lips and rubs his hands together. I follow him into the kitchen.

"*Preparemos unas tortillas,*" he says.

Abuelito puts a plastic bag called "*Masa Harina de Maíz*—Corn Masa Mix" on the counter. He turns on the faucet and moistens his hands. "*Agua,*" he says.

"Water," I say, and wet my fingers too. We scoop our hands into the bag of flour. I pound the dough with my fist and squish it on the counter. I make a face with a big nose and long eyelashes. Abuelito adds a skinny mustache.

"*Mira*," Abuelito says and points with his chin. He rolls the dough into a little ball, patting it against one palm and then the other, making a flat circle. "*Uno, dos, tres*," he counts.

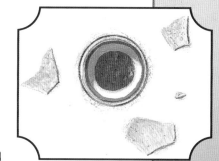

"Four, five, six," I continue, and soon my stomach is talking again.

Abuelito puts our round circles in a frying pan. He shows me how to flip them over to the other side when they sizzle. Abuelito puffs up his cheeks and when the tortillas get puffy, too, he scoops them out and lays them in a basket lined with a cloth.

"*Delicioso*," Abuelito says, taking a bite.

"*Mmmmm*," I agree and reach for another one.

Abuelito melts some cheese in the pan and pours it over the tortillas. Then we dip them in the red sauce Abuelito calls "*salsa*." I burp and Abuelito burps louder.

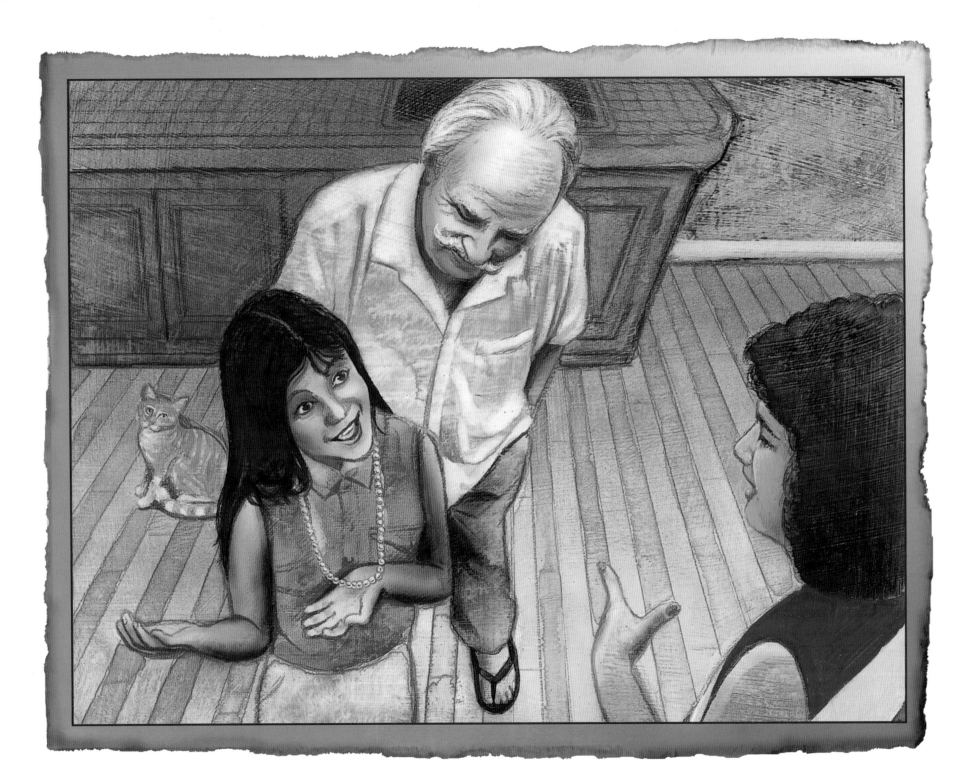

When my mother comes back, she points to the dishes in the sink. "What have you two been up to?" she asks.

"Abuelito gave me a necklace and the *santos* switched places and I can count in Spanish and *guess what?* Abuelito eats with his fingers and so do I."

My mother laughs and hugs Abuelito goodbye. I squeeze in the middle between them. My grandfather kisses my forehead and tucks the sketchpad under my arm. He wipes some sauce off my chin.

"*Dios te bendiga,*" he blesses me.

On the way home, I decide to draw a picture
of Abuelito's block, with a man in a straw hat and a
woman with long, dark hair.

I will show Hope my pearl necklace, but I won't let
her borrow it.

She has her own
grandfather to visit.

About Author Janice Levy

Janice Levy has taught English as a second language and Spanish and traveled extensively through Hispanic countries. This is her fifth picture book. She is the author of *The Spirit of Tío Fernando*, a bilingual Day of the Dead story about a child's spiritual search. It was a commended title in the 1995 Américas Award for Children and Young Adult Literature. *Abuelito Goes Home* is part of a nationwide elementary school reading program. *Totally Uncool* is a humorous story of a child's relationship with her father's girlfriend. It won Honorable Mention in the 1996 *Writer's Digest* Magazine Writing Competition. *Abuelito Eats With His Fingers* won Second Place in the 1996 *Writer's Digest* Magazine Writing Competition.

Ms. Levy's adult fiction has been published in nationally acclaimed anthologies and magazines. In 1998, her work won First Place in the *Writer's Digest* Magazine Writing Competition.

Ms. Levy lives in New York with her husband, Rick, children, Michael and Jahnna, and Zöe the Wonder Dog. She has loving memories of her grandfather, who also ate with his fingers.

About Illustrator Layne Johnson

Born and raised in Houston, Texas, Layne has worked as an illustrator for the last 16 years. He enjoys many interests, including raquetball, woodworking, and maintaining his small grape vineyard.

"My son Brett loves to visit his grandparents. He will have many fond memories like helping his Mommom make Christmas cookies, and building things with his Poppop. Brett has grown up eating as many grapes, plums and pears as he could get with his country grandparents, his Ma Maw and Pa Paw. Without much persuasion, they often take Brett fishing.

"These are all priceless memories. It is a gift to realize how special grandparents really are."